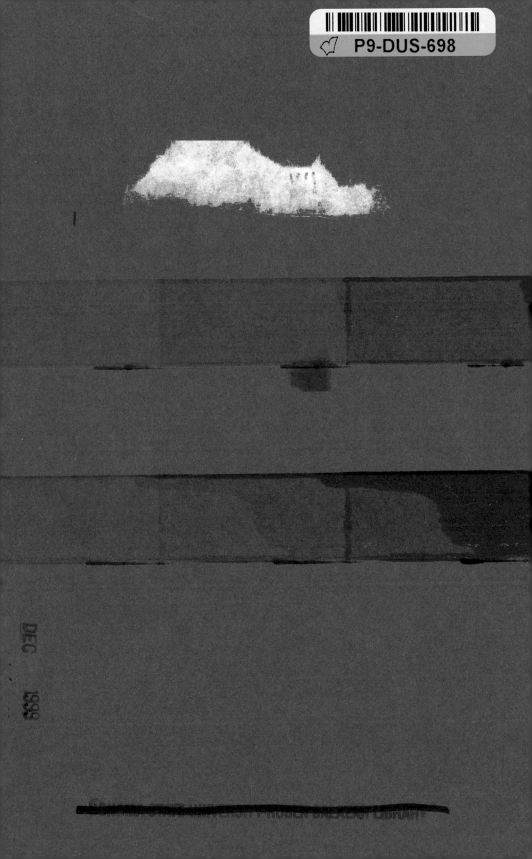

A Note to Parents

Welcome to REAL KIDS READERS, a series of phonics-based books for children who are beginning to read. In the classroom, educators use phonics to teach children how to sound out unfamiliar words, providing a firm foundation for reading skills. At home, you can use REAL KIDS READERS to reinforce and build on that foundation, because the books follow the same basic phonic guidelines that children learn in school.

Of course the best way to help your child become a good reader is to make the experience fun—and REAL KIDS READERS do that, too. With their realistic story lines and lively characters, the books engage children's imaginations. With their clean design and sparkling photographs, they provide picture clues that help new readers decipher the text. The combination is sure to entertain young children and make them truly want to read.

REAL KIDS READERS have been developed at three distinct levels to make it easy for children to read at their own pace.

- LEVEL 1 is for children who are just beginning to read.
- LEVEL 2 is for children who can read with help.
- LEVEL 3 is for children who can read on their own.

A controlled vocabulary provides the framework at each level. Repetition, rhyme, and humor help increase word skills. Because children can understand the words and follow the stories, they quickly develop confidence. They go back to each book again and again, increasing their proficiency and sense of accomplishment, until they're ready to move on to the next level. The result is a rich and rewarding experience that will help them develop a lifelong love of reading.

For my mom
—S. H.

Special thanks to Hanna Andersson, Portland, OR, for
providing clothing and to Converse for providing sneakers.

Produced by DWAI / Seventeenth Street Productions, Inc.
Reading Specialist: Virginia Grant Clammer

Library of Congress Cataloging-in-Publication Data
Hood, Susan.
   The new kid / Susan Hood ; photographs by Dorothy Handelman.
      p.   cm. — (Real kids readers. Level 1)
   Summary: The new boy in class is a disruptive pest until one child remembers how bad it
feels to be new at school and makes friends with Sid.
   ISBN 0-7613-2014-8 (lib. bdg.). — ISBN 0-7613-2039-3 (pbk.)
   [1. Friendship—Fiction. 2. Behavior—Fiction. 3. Schools—Fiction. 4. Stories in rhyme.]
I. Handelman, Dorothy, ill. II. Title. III. Series.
PZ8.3.H7577Ng 1998
[E]—dc21   98-10040
                                                                                CIP
                                                                                AC

pbk: 10 9 8 7 6 5 4 3 2 1
lib: 10 9 8 7 6 5 4 3 2 1

The New Kid

By Susan Hood
Photographs by Dorothy Handelman

M
The Millbrook Press
Brookfield, Connecticut

One day in the fall,
in class with Miss Hall,

4

TODAY IS
MONDAY
OCTOBER 7

WEATHER

a new kid comes in.
I look up and grin.

He sits down with me,
with Bess, and with Lee.

The new boy is Sid.
He is silly, that kid!

Sid likes to blab.
Sid likes to grab.

We all do our best.
But Sid is a pest.

He makes a mess.
He spills on Bess!

Miss Hall gets mad
when Sid acts bad.

19

I think he is sad,
and so he acts bad.

21

I was sad too
when I was new.

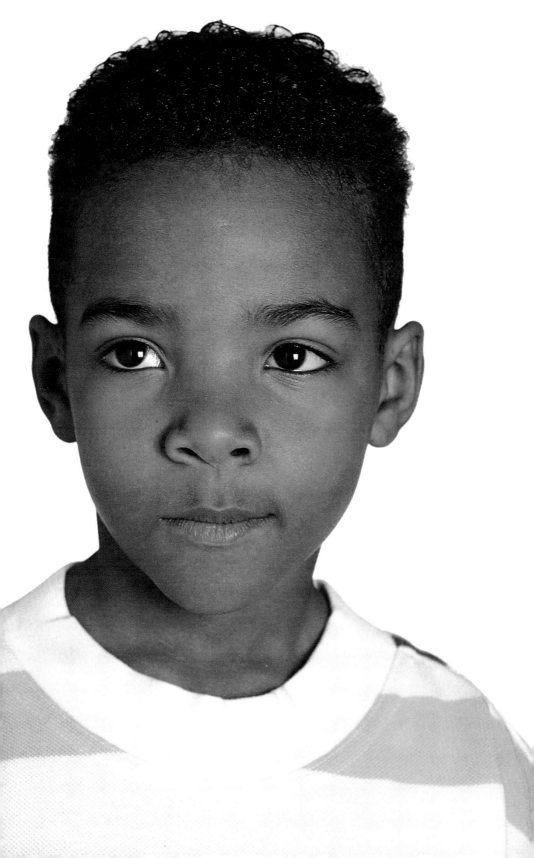

I ask Sid to play.
He says okay.

25

We jump and we run.
We have lots of fun.

Now Sid is not sad.
He does not act bad.

Boy, are we glad!

31

Reading with Your Child

1. Try to read with your child at least twenty minutes each day, as part of your regular routine.
2. Keep your child's books in one convenient, cozy reading spot.
3. Read and familiarize yourself with the Phonic Guidelines below.
4. Ask your child to read *The New Kid* out loud. If he or she has difficulty with a word:
   - Help him or her decode the word phonetically. (Say, "Try to sound it out.")
   - Encourage him or her to use picture clues. (Say, "What does the picture show?")
   - Ask him or her to use context clues. (Say, "What would make sense?")
5. If your child still doesn't "get" the word, tell him or her what it is. Don't wait for frustration to build.
6. Praise your beginning reader. With your enthusiasm and encouragement, your child will go from one success to the next.

Phonic Guidelines

Use the following guidelines to help your child read the words in *The New Kid*.

Short Vowels

When two consonants surround a vowel, the sound of the vowel is usually short. This means you pronounce *a* as in apple, *e* as in egg, *i* as in igloo, *o* as in octopus, and *u* as in umbrella. Short-vowel words in this story include: *bad, but, fun, gets, kid, lots, mad, not, run, sad, Sid, sits.*

Short-Vowel Words with Beginning Consonant Blends

When two different consonants begin a word, they usually blend to make a combined sound. Words in this story with beginning consonant blends include: *blab, class, glad, grab, grin, spills.*

Short-Vowel Words with Ending Consonant Blends

When two different consonants end a word, they usually blend to make a combined sound. Words in this story with ending consonant blends include: *act, ask, best, jump, pest.*

Double Consonants

When two of the same consonants are side by side, one of them is silent. In this story, double consonants appear in the short-vowel words *Bess, mess,* and *Miss,* and in the *all*-family words *all, fall, Hall.*

Sight Words

Sight words are those words that a reader must learn to recognize immediately—by sight—instead of by sounding them out. They occur with high frequency in easy texts. Sight words not included in the above categories are: *a, and, are, boy, comes, day, do, down, have, he, I, in, is, likes, look, makes, me, new, now, of, on, one, our, play, says, so, that, the, think, to, too, up, was, we, when, with.*